JACARANDA BLUES

Mehreen Ahmed

PublishAmerica
Baltimore

First printing

Softcover 9781462640904
PUBLISHED BY PUBLISHAMERICA, LLLP
www.publishamerica.com
Baltimore

Printed in the United States of America

JACARANDA
BLUES

Episode 1

'What's with Sam?' Rhonda cogitated one summer morning as she sat down on the bench under the Jacaranda tree contemplating the events of last night; the huge argument that she had with her partner Sam! 'What's his problem? He loses his temper at a drop of a hat these days!' What was it she said that ticked him so? All she ever said was, `You've become too irritable lately,' and he nearly broke a glass over it!

At fifty-two Rhonda Smith had a figure of a teenager. Her curves compensated for the woodenness of the flat chest and this morning her red, tweed skirt hung modestly around the pinched waist, accentuating the loveliness of the waist line while the white chiffon blouse hugged her milky soft skin desperately. She wore red lipstick and slight mascara which took the paleness away but did not hide the very first signs of wrinkles beginning to appear along the peripheries of her thin lips; a cluster of hairline crows feet in the corner of her large brown eyes, grew deeper with every smile.

But alas it was futile! She derived no solace from the splendor of the Jacaranda tree which looked serene enough in the freshness of the summer's morning as thousands of lilac petals blazed in the breeze. Her eyes squinted slightly to absorb its brightness against the sky's bluish Mediterranean tinge but that was all. Given, that the tree didn't exactly stand in any secret garden but the most unromantic of places right in the middle of a busy street across the bus stop, next to the café near Rhonda's place, it was a sight quite serendipitous for nature lovers'! And she was one of them!

When the bus arrived she got up from the bench still engrossed in her thoughts. A Mercedes was parked on the curb as she scanned the road to walk across; a well built middle aged man of medium height got out of the car. He looked towards the direction of the café. Rhonda proceeded towards the bus-stop, stepped onto the bus and looked out of the window. The gentleman was heading for the café and by now there was another man in his early twenties who sat down under the tree to read. The bus took off! But her thoughts played havoc within as life around her continued uneventfully peaceful, normal.

The bus stopped in front of the hospital where she worked as admin about fifteen minutes earlier than usual. Rhonda descended and walked slowly into the building. On her way to her office she said hello to nurse Lisa who was pushing a stretcher trolley along into the operation theatre in a real hurry. She entered her office calmly into the rooms of the specialist general practitioner, no 202. Suddenly, she was all wet again with hot flushes and sweats springing up her shoulders and onto her face. Quickly she went into the toilet, dabbed the sweat off and applied fresh make-up. The phone rang, she paid no attention; it rang out. It rang again! This time she sat down at her desk and answered it.

"Dr Burton's office, Rhonda speaking."

"Yes, this is Haley, Haley Longbottom."

"Hi, Haley, how're you?"

"Good, thanks. I was actually calling to cancel tomorrow's appointment?"

"Yes, of course. It was at 2:30, wasn't it?" Rhonda asked as she scrolled down the computer screen.

"Yes. I'll call back to reschedule it."

"Yeah! That's fine!"

"Thanks, bye."

"Bye, Hailey." She hung up.

Rhonda then decided to clear her desk and the drawers. She did so intermittently, over the calls.

It has been ages since she's done it and before Christmas this year, she thought she must. The incredible amount of rubbish that piled up over the years! She kept thinking as she went through scraps of paper, a temple bar from an old pair of sun glasses and a whole lot of knick knacks good-for-nothing stuff, trash that ends up in the drawers from God-knows-where. In the midst of all this, Rhonda suddenly found a small treasure box stashed away down in the back of the drawer. And as she opened it there was a crumpled piece of paper that had a phone number and a name, `Chris' boldly written on it. She toyed with the idea thinking exactly how long has it been since he had given this to her, begging her to call him! Thirty years? Nearly three decades! Almost as long as she's been working here! She reminisced. Looking back, it felt strange how she met Sam a year after and married him. She didn't give Chris or herself for that matter, even half a chance to find out how life could have been otherwise! And now? Their relationship! Sam's and hers, is on the rocks. She looked at the yellowish, crumpled, torn piece of paper and wondered if this number is still his … after all these years!

Should she call him? Rhonda couldn't decide. She might try after work perhaps! That's when he'll be at home. But what would she say to him? She began to have stomach pains at the mere thought of it, a lingering, uneasy, dull kind. She nearly chucked it away scrunching it up between her fingers into the palm of her hand. But no, wait! She looked at the ball of craggy piece of paper, put it back on her desk and then ironed it out with those very fingers that tried to crush it. He might be married by now! Or could be with somebody else! Then there was Sam. The phone rang piercing through her thoughts like a sharp blade.

It was lunch time. She took her book out of the hand bag as she put Chris's number inside making her way slowly towards the hospital café. Her usual spot was gone today so she sat at a different table with her Chicken and a Lettuce sandwich and a cup of English breakfast tea. Opening her book in the middle of *Virginia Woolf's Mrs Dalloway,* she settled down in her own cocoon. Her favorite subject at school was English and that's where she acquired the taste for classics but she never made it to the university. She found a strange affinity between herself and Clarissa Dalloway. Her dilemmas were most fascinating much like hers, especially these days.

"And what was it that made her marry Sam?" she muttered.

He had swept her off her feet at the time. Yes, now she remembers! It's all coming back to her, his composure, the stability that he stood for, the promise of a secure life. Whereas, Chris's bohemian lifestyle always put her off; she did not think it was good for marriage. At the time she made a decision, a sensible one in which love might or might not have had a role to play. What was more appealing was a promise of a peaceful life, the pristine life that she has had until now …untouched by quandary! But that too, was slipping away and she was powerless to recapture it, a virtuous relationship, and its limpidness that knew neither quarrels nor deceit. The consummation didn't even lead to an offspring, a problem that Rhonda had that the doctors couldn't fix. Life with Chris could have been exotic perhaps but complex, and she didn't have the courage to embark on it; she let it go into oblivion.

She had met Chris on a train station. Rhonda literally bumped onto him as she was about to get on it one spring afternoon on her way to the public library in the city. She had a huge pile of fat books in her arms which fell scattered all over the platform and as she stepped back to collect them, she suddenly realized that she was not alone. In the meantime, the train slowly pushed away.

"Hi! I am Chris," he had said beaming. "Sorry about this. The next train won't be long. Are you in a hurry?"

Wow, Chris was a bit of a talker. Rhonda thought, but she liked him. There was a kind debonair recklessness about him which she couldn't ignore.

"Oh! Thanks," she had said. "Actually, I do have some time."

"Would you like to go for a coffee? My shout!"

"Oh, okay!"

And they had hopped across the road together heading for the café. They had so much to talk about that it surprised Rhonda. They talked endlessly about art, literature and music.

A cleaner for a mum and a mad punter for a dad, mum had been in and out of relationships ever since his sudden disappearance one day. And because of this misfortune, Rhonda did not have much luck with education; she needed to chip in once in a while to make ends meet for the family of four. Her siblings would have gone astray otherwise, if she hadn't done her job at her gay Uncle Tom's shop called, 'Fresh Fruits and Vegetables.' Her sisters and brother were not doing too badly now working in the same place, putting vegetables on the shelves. But Rhonda always knew that she was different! She liked reading and did well in literature class. Her English teacher always encouraged her to study literature at the university but she needed money … badly! And a university education would have been a waste of time for her, a mockery! So, after grade twelve she chose to do an administrative course instead. She hadn't particularly loved this job but it gave her the financial security and some social status.

Chris talked about George Orwell and Rhonda had read *The Animal farm*. One cup of coffee led to lunch, trains came and went by but they couldn't care less. He had then taken her home at sun down, exchanged phone numbers promising to meet her again at the entrance of her mother's house.

He had called her one evening to take her out to dinner and Rhonda had her best clothes on. It was a short navy blue skirt with a pink top with plunging neckline. They went to the cheap end of Valley. It had not mattered what they ate, fish and chips, but the romance had been unbelievable! That was Rhonda's first date; she had the blush of a partly opened bud just before flowering into full bloom. After dinner Chris had sat next to her holding her hand on the bench as they waited for the bus. And then slowly … oh, how very gently! He had brought his head down to her full red lips and kissed her under the lamp post which she had returned with the same fervor! Eventually, the bus came and they got on, not knowing though which way they were heading and then suddenly Chris asked.

"How about my place! For a nightcap."

"Sure thing!"

Rhonda had agreed feeling quite dizzy from the heady romance fanned by Chris's heavy breathing. The storm that was seen looming in the afternoon had started no sooner had they reached his house. The rain had simply unleashed itself from the dark clouds with thunder heralding as though Prometheus was free at last lightening the heavens with the stolen fire! Unbound!

They had entered the house and lit a cozy fire in the fire place of the living room. Chris had given Rhonda one of his shirts and a towel to wipe off. And as she was about to, there were two other helping hands on her shoulders which were now traveling below her waist; Chris was pulling down the zipper of the skirt with his firm, able hands and Rhonda went along with it! He let it fall on the floor and then taking the towel from her hand wiped her back first and then her bottom, pressing it lightly as he went on. He then turned her around without a word, looked at her soft ear lobes momentarily before he bent down to kiss them. He barely touched them with his lips, nibbled them gently between his teeth and all the way down to her neck. In the soft glow of the crackling fire her tender lips looked luscious than ever as the towel approached her breasts, Rhonda stood very still, not knowing what to do next but her heart raced away faster than the lightening of the skies. Moments passed before it happened, her very first love-making! The top was gone and the bra strap had come undone! Before she even realized, she was lying somehow on the floor next to the fire with his lips caressing and brushing every bit of her yielding body in hot pursuit. The storm had finally passed; the thunder and the lightening eased off too. It was nearly two in the morning when both woke up to raid the fridge with ravenous hunger.

Episode 2

Rhonda never regretted it! To get her bearing, she sat once again on her way home under the Jacaranda tree as she got off the bus after work. The happy memories came flooding back with awful clarity. She wished! And then she did not wish, for this to happen but it was happening! That phone number was still inside her bag. She played with the idea as to what might happen after all these years if she really were to call him. Would she have the guts then to speak to him or simply hang up? But the situation is now altered; marriage has made such a big difference hasn't it? Time had brushed her too but the heart still remained passionately young. Had she slept walk through life? The sudden realization of her existence, this rather permanent temporariness and how she failed to utilize it suddenly struck her at the very core. She felt, she was not only beginning to wake up but also ready to fall in love again, start all over and give it another go. And Chris! What of Chris? Could he give her a taste of the heavenly joy, that happiness she craved so much but never really found?

Dinner was already under way. Sam was at home when she opened the door. Her siblings were having dinner with them that evening. Sam was a good cook when he was in a good mood, and today was one of those days; the corridor to their apartment was filled with the aromas of his cooking. Rhonda turned the key to unlock the door.

"There you are! Finally," Sam greeted her with a smile. "How's work?"

"O, the usual!" Rhonda said sliding the hand bag off her shoulders with her long tapering fingers and putting it on the sofa as he put the roasting pan in the oven.

"When did you get in?" she asked.

"About an hour and a half."

"Good, good!" she said. "Have you put the laundry out?"

"Yes, I have," he replied grimly.

Rhonda looked at him briefly and felt a sudden drop in the temperature.

"You have done it again! I told you so many times to not to mix my clothes with yours. You don't seem to be paying much attention at all!"

"Well there weren't enough clothes of my own even for a small load. I needed to do the laundry pretty bad!" Rhonda answered.

"Couldn't you wait for a day or two? Also, I couldn't find the pots and the pans in the right place. You can't do anything right. You seem to be getting disorganized by the day."

How his intonation suddenly changed! His voice started to get higher and higher to the point of yelling...so horrible that the heart could stop. Rhonda quickly escaped into the bathroom. The last thing she wanted was another fight over pots and pans and laundry! Their guests would be arriving soon any way.

In the shower she thought of the changes in her life. She could not stop thinking of Chris! He was training to be a doctor, where does he work? The warmth of the hot shower seemed to relax her a bit. She turned it off and wrapped herself with the bath towel hanging down the bracket behind the door. She heard voices coming from the other room. They were already here, she thought, and early! Quickly she grabbed whatever dress she found in her closet, off the hanger. It was a white dress with huge purple flowers, then ran a comb through her short layered hair, dabbed a bit of pink lipstick, pressed the thin lips together and zipped out of the room.

"Hello everyone!"

She smiled at them brightly before sliding her feet into a pair of summer sandals sitting beside the sofa in the living room. Her two sisters, Emily and Clara sat next to each other and David, her brother, on the far end of the sofa.

"Dinner is nearly ready."

Sam said smiling again handing them each a 4X Beer.

"Thanks!"

"So? What's new?" Rhonda asked dropping herself into a nearby bean bag.

"Oh! Not much, business is as usual at the store," David scowled. We haven't got our raise yet!"

"How awful!" Rhonda exclaimed. "Have you asked for it though?"

"No, not in so many words, but we have expressed our interest."

"These things take time!" Sam said.

He looked over his shoulder as he pulled the rack of the lamb out of the oven putting it on the table.

"Yes, but not even a single raise in five years, that sucks!" Rhonda said.

"I agree! But do you have any idea how hard it is to run a vegetable store?" Sam barked at Rhonda. "You sit in your cozy little office answering phones all day, what would you know about the world outside?"

"And I' s'pose you do! I know more about green grocers than you could ever imagine!"

"Then why aren't you one! If you knew so much?"

This absurd debate was going to ruin dinner, Rhonda thought as she got up to set the table. She took the plates, the cutlery, and the glasses out of the kitchen cabinet and put them on the table without a word while her siblings exchanged quick confused looks.

"Dinner's been served," Rhonda muttered.

The spread wasn't all that bad. There was the lamb rack, boiled mixed vegetables, corn on the cob stuffed roasted chicken and dinner rolls. Sam opened a bottle of red sparkling wine and poured some into everyone's glass as they all sat around the table. While Rhonda took her seat opposite Sam, Clara and Emily sat next to each other as always and David opposite to them. Clara who was a big eater took a generous helping of everything, whereas, Emily only took a small slice of the lamb and some corn on the cob. David on the other hand had a full meal.

"Emily, aren't you well? You haven't eaten much!" Sam said.

"I'm fine. Thanks. I am really not that hungry," she said.

Rhonda thought miserably that even she hasn't got much of an appetite either. Thanks to you for spoiling it!

Clara's lavish compliments didn't go unnoticed as she took a second helping. Sam ate quite well, Rhonda thought, looking at him over the rim of her wine glass as she lifted it up. The arguments didn't seem to affect him much at all.

"I nearly got run over in the car, the other day," Emily said.

"Goodness me! How?" Rhonda exclaimed.

"O, nothing terrible happened just this car in front was

weaving in and out between lanes. He came too close to the bumper bar of my car and hit it. We pulled over and exchanged details. My car hasn't gone to the mechanics yet, still getting quotes," she said. "It happened on Centennial highway towards Ipswich. The driver of the other vehicle was a lad, 17 at the most."

There was a bit of a difference in age between Rhonda and her Siblings. David was now 34, Clara 40 and Emily 44. All single, none could hold a relationship.

"He was driving a BMW convertible, his dad's!"

Clara said who was also in the car with Emily.

"He was very apologetic afterwards and did mention something about getting into trouble with dad!"

"Pity, it wasn't a write-off," observed David.

"Well, thank God! There could have been serious injuries. Have you thought of that?" Clara blurted out.

"Trying to make a little money on the sly, hey David?" Sam said.

"That's our David!" added Clara.

And David just smiled to all of that. This conversation was

making Rhonda a bit uncomfortable as she exchanged glances with Emily. Sam didn't know but David was once caught for nicking money from the till. Luckily, he was pardoned, at the time, because he was under aged.

Dinner was finished and they each put the dishes in the dishwasher. Rhonda waited near the sink until all the dishes were in and Sam put out the dessert with plates and dessert forks. Clara put the kettle to the boil for tea. The water in the kettle started to boil in minutes. She took the cups and saucers to the table, milk and sugar. Emily liked chocolate milk. Apart from her everyone else had Earl Grey. Each bag was dunked into the tea cups and steaming boiled water poured into them. David took two sugars, Clara one sugar and milk while Rhonda and Sam had theirs black.

"What's on tele?" Emily asked suddenly.

"Kath and Kim," Sam said flicking the remote to turn it on.

"Our uncle has broken up with his lover, did you know?"

David asked looking at Rhonda.

"About bloody time! He has been with that jerk for donkey's years!" Rhonda said.

"Yes! But do you know over what, though?" Clara asked. "He claimed a share of the shop for putting all those years into the relationship."

Sam suddenly seemed all ears into the conversation. Family matters didn't interest him of late.

"Really! And Uncle Tom kicked him out like a pair of old shoes?" Sam chimed in.

"No, I don't think it was that easy. I heard arguments coming out of his office one day as I was stacking up boxes on the shelf," David said. "And the next thing was that there was a thumping noise. Shortly afterwards, Jim was seen opening the door with a bloody nose and he was gone; out of the shop and hopefully out of his life."

The evening rolled as the gossip ended and Rhonda felt tired. Her siblings left and she kissed them goodbye as she and Sam, both saw them out. She turned on the dishwasher yawning, went into the bathroom to brush her teeth. Sam was already there so she decided to get changed first in the walk-in closet. She had just barely taken her dress off and she felt a caress on her back. Sam was running his index finger up and down her torso and then slowly into the hips. She turned around to give him a kiss. They kissed on the lips, cheeks and then slid their tongues into each others mouth. They were making out on the carpet inside the walk-in closet, next to the bed.

Rhonda was able to get up finally to brush her teeth. She went to bed after that with Sam. He started to snore in no time, but she couldn't sleep. She quietly got up, opened the door softly and went into the study. Her photo album was sitting on the heaps of books in one corner of the floor. She picked it up and flicked through the pages. It hurt to see how her youth was gone! Down the memory lane! Her thoughts drifted away to the elderly lady that she saw on the bus today, her wrinkly hands and her face. She thought of death…she thought of it a lot! And now, she was gradually dozing off on the carpet there, didn't even have the strength to walk back to bed.

Episode 3

The phone rang first thing in the morning. 'God! Who could that be?' Rhonda thought squinting at the sun light streaming through the window. She slept in the study last night. Her neck hurt. She scuffled out of the blanket somehow and reached for the phone. Sam came around in the early hours of the morning and covered her with a white and red check cotton blanket. No, too late! It rang out! She was awake now but she couldn't stop thinking about Chris! No matter how hard she tried. 'Do you think you could turn my world upside down?' She thought as she looked at herself objectively for the first time in the vanity mirror of her bathroom! No! She decided this can't be; this can not be the face that Chris would fall in love with all over again. It simply wouldn't work! Then why can't she get him out of her mind? She looked closely at her lips and yes! She found traces of wrinkles on the upper lip. This is her life now, her new life and she must teach herself to live with it. At least she had her books! No one can take those away! And of course she must read!

The phone rang again. This time she hurried out of the toilet and picked it up.

"Hello, Rhonda speaking."

"Yes!" a deep male voice said. "This number was given to me by Clara, Clara Smith, may I speak to her please?"

"Clara, doesn't live here," Rhonda answered. "I'm her sister Rhonda."

"O! This was her contact number. Would you be able to give her a message for me please?" he asked.

"Yes, of course," Rhonda said.

"My name is Chris. Dr. Chris Saunders. I believe my son and your sister were in a crash. I don't know if you are aware of it. Could you ask her to meet me? I would like to discuss the matter over with her first."

Rhonda's heart started to pound as though somebody was hammering it! Her head throbbed so! She thought she was going to faint! She could barely speak.

"Chris! Do I know you? This is Rhonda, Rhonda Smith," she managed.

"Rhonda Smith? Rhonda! It does ring a bell, although it's been awhile," Chris's smooth voice cut through the mouth piece of the phone. "Are you the same person that I went out with? The same Rhonda?"

"Yes! Yes!" Rhonda said breathing heavily.

"Really? Unbelievable!"

"You haven't for-forgotten then!"

"No, no of course not! How could I? And how have you been?" he said.

"O,Good … good, good."

She said it with a huge effort to stay calm.

"It's been so long! Do you want to meet one day?" he asked.

"Um! Sure! …W-When? Where?"

"How about the Valley? Where it all started!"

"Sure! When?"

"Friday evening at 5 `O' clock?" he asked.

"Yeah, I'll get off work early."

"See you then!" he said.

"See you."

She couldn't think straight she felt her heart was going to

leap out of her throat any time.

"Bye," he said.

"Bye."

Do not get overwhelmed Rhonda Smith! She repeated over and over again breathing deeply at the same time. She had butterflies in her stomach, her hands trembled and she couldn't find Sam in the flat that morning. He must have gone out for a jog, she thought. She made herself a cup of tea with shaky hands and took it out on the balcony of the quiet morning. She looked up against the gentle breeze and saw larks flying about in the tranquil blue sky. She whispered, 'O, Chris, what on earth compelled you to show up! We are late, oh, so late, 20 years too late!' She thought of Chris's son and his mother whom he must have fallen in love with at some stage and then married her. Where is Rhonda's place in all this? She wished her soul aged too, as did her body! She wished she stopped loving him!

Sam was back from his jog. He saw her in the balcony went in and gave her a peck on the shoulder before he stepped into the shower. Friday was just two days away and the mere thought of it gave her the cramps! She would have to deal with it … some how! Sam sat down for breakfast later on but Rhonda seemed in a real hurry. She couldn't eat anything.

"What's wrong?" Sam asked

"I'll grab something at the hospital."

She picked up her black bag lying on the sofa next to the dining table. Sam was showing signs of age as she looked at his profile. The dark receding hairline was graying with a salt and pepper look. The blue eyes looked sallow and the freckled long nose above the narrow lips looked somewhat bigger. While his mustache was black and white, there were quite a few character lines that appeared on the forehead and on the roundish surface of his cheeks. She kissed him goodbye on the forehead and shut the door behind her with a soft thump as she left.

Episode 4

It didn't take that long for Friday to arrive and the two days went by without much ado. Rhonda could not eat well, sleep well! Her days were filled with thoughts she couldn't block. Even *Mrs Dalloway* failed to amuse her ... keep her steadfast. She went over the 'dos' and the 'don'ts' a thousand times in her mind. Oh! This wait ... these horrible, slothful moments were going to give her a few more wrinkles and a few more grey hair, she pondered. But soon the moments passed and the day arrived.

Sam woke up early as usual for his morning jog. Rhonda slept in purposely waiting for him to leave. She was fully aware of Sam going into the toilet. She heard the flush and then out he came. Sam put his jog suit on and tied his shoe laces and kissed Rhonda good bye on the forehead thinking how pretty she still looked in the morning sun. Rhonda did not move her eyelid even a fraction when all this happened. She heard Sam open and close the door.

Rhonda got out of bed. She must! Yes, she must look her best today...her absolute best! She stumbled on her bedroom slippers as she put them on and went into the toilet. Then she looked if the hair color had hidden all her greys properly . No, she couldn't find a single one in her short, brown hair. Her skin looked smooth with all the anti aging cream that she had been applying. Today she applied a bit more. Rhonda brushed her teeth and then went into the shower. Picking a dress afterwards was the hardest. She was going to go to work first so it had to be smart casual, not too gaudy… not that she liked gaudy. She chose a bright red ankle skirt with a multi-colored floral blouse. She must be gone before Sam gets in! So, as fast as she could, Rhonda got the cereal box out of the cabinet and the milk from the fridge slid the rolled oats into the little black bowl and poured some milk over it. Then she opened the drawer to fetch a table spoon. Sam would be home anytime now; she could hear her own heart beat. She would have to own up to him one day for this act but that day can wait! For now, she must write a note!

She left the note on the counter top, reached for her black bag and dabbed a bit of pink lipstick on her thin pale lips; she inhaled a deep breath as her hand took the door knob and turned it to open and close the door behind her. Down the corridor and then the stairs off she went towards the bus stop. She didn't realize however, that Sam was returning and was close enough to see her leave in those hasty steps.

Sitting under the Jacaranda tree as usual waiting for the bus, she was having difficulty breathing. As she looked towards the café she caught a glimpse of a car … a red car, a Toyota sedan. There was a little boy of about three years of age sitting in the car seat. Nothing out of the ordinary but the couple in the car was about Rhonda's age. The lady parked the car on the side of the road near the café and got out of her seat. Once she was out, she then opened the back door and took the child out of his car seat. The boy was asleep but something about him, something that she could not quite put her finger on. Was he in a hospital? He looked quite pale and bony almost mal nourished! Children of that age didn't usually look that way

The bus was here and Rhonda got on paying the driver and settling down in her cozy window seat. The couple with the child got up too. By now the child was awake and Rhonda saw his cadaverous look. His eyes were rather large and black which were heightened by his curly black hair right above the forehead. This darkness about him gave him a pallor that subdued his olive skin color. They sat down two seats away from Rhonda behind the driver. The boy looked at Rhonda and smiled at her weakly before he turned his eyes away. The couple pressed the stop button to get off at the bus stop, and Rhonda looked around to see if she could find anything significant about this place. This was High Gate Hill and apart from an old orphanage situated within a church, there was nothing else. The couple hopped off, the bus started to move and Rhonda's stop was next. As she walked towards the hospital, she was preoccupied with her meeting with Chris but at the same time the child's image … his sickly large black eyes emerged mindlessly.

Sam entered the flat. He closed the door behind him and walked over to the sink to get a glass of water from the tap.

Rhonda left the milk bottle on the countertop with the lid lying around with her half eaten cereal bowl next to it. There was also a folded note on the countertop with Sam's name written on it. He cursed softly as he put the lid back on the bottle and put it back in the fridge.

With sweat dripping all over his body he picked up the note as he drained the cereal bowl into the sink. The note said, "I'll be late, don't wait up for me." 'What's in the world going on? She never tells me anything anymore!'

Ever since Sam got a sack from the hardware store at Bunnings, he was unable to find work. Rhonda was happy for him to just stay home and do the chores, run errands and the rest of it. Sam felt restless at times but slowly learn't to enjoy the quiet life. Rhonda earned enough for their upkeep; everything fell nicely in place.

As soon as he hit the shower, the mobile rang. It rang for a while and then stopped and when he got out he picked it up … one missed call. David. 'What's he up to?' The towel still wrapped around him he called David. He picked it up instantly.

“I’m at the police station!” he screamed.

“What! How come?” Sam asked.

“Can you come down to the police station now? I’ll explain!”

“Which one?”

“Blacktown.”

“Sure thing! I’ll be there in half an hour.”

He quickly got changed as he thought,‘what’s he done? Has he gone mad? Or has the world gone mad? David! In the police station! I better call Rhonda.’

Episode 5

Rhonda was at her desk answering phones when the mobile rang. 'It must be Chris,' she thought …'can't stay away clearly as she couldn't!' She opened her bag, delved her unsteady hands deep in it rummaging through the many things and dug it out. 'It's Sam!'

Her voice quivered in panic as she picked it up.

"Hello?"

"Sorry Darl?" David's just called, said he's in the police station," there was urgency in his voice. "I'm on my way there now; can you get off for a couple of hours?"

Rhonda knew something was wrong. David had a track record of stealing money from the till and was pardoned at the time for being a minor. No one told Sam about it because it was too embarrassing! But it was out now! No use trying to hush it up, not anymore.

"Hello, are you still there?" Sam asked.

"Yes! Yes, just thinking what to do? Why don't you let me

deal with it, I'll go and you stay home," Rhonda said.

Sam should not, under any circumstances, be allowed to go to the police station. She didn't trust him with family secrets. Rhonda would then have to endure his self righteous, judgmental lectures all her life.

"Okay! If you say so but I'm telling you it's bloody serious!" he said.

"O, look! I'm sure it is just a little mischief that he's got himself into," Rhonda ended.

"No worries," he said

"No worries."

Rhonda smiled, thinking that she's been able to pull this one off quite well. They both hung up. At least she had Chris to share this burden with. Oh! What a relief! Rhonda called David and David told her everything! Same old, same old! Except that this time he stole a much bigger amount and over many days! Accounts showed that nearly two thousand dollars went missing from David's till. He buckled under pressure at the police station during the interview but this time there was going to be heavy penalty, undoubtedly. On lunch Rhonda walked straight to the bus stop. She had her black bag over her shoulder as she took the bus bound for Blacktown police station.

At the police station, David sat looking eagerly out of the French windows for Rhonda. When he finally saw him, his heart leapt with joy as Rhonda walked into the station and went straight to the police officer sitting at the desk. She had a glimpse of David from where he was seated, in the corner of the room, slightly away from the sliding door. As soon as he saw her, he got up and followed her to stand next to her at the reception; Rhonda turned sideways to look at him.

"O David! What have you got yourself into this time," she exclaimed.

"Big trouble I'm afraid," David said.

"I'll take care of it, darling! Don't you worry!" Rhonda reassured.

"I'll never do it again, I promise."

"May I help you?" the police officer asked. She had a white starched blouse on and a navy blue skirt. Her brown lipstick stood out on her thick lips tightly shut together in a smile that looked more like a grimace. Cold, clear and professional, her voice carried the message across the desk while she sat at the computer looking at the screen.

"Yes," Rhonda said in voice that matched hers. "I'm David's sister. I was asked to come."

"There's has been an AVO placed against David."

She said it nonchalantly pulling up David's record on the screen.

"By whom?" Rhonda asked.

"By Tom Smith," the police officer confirmed looking at the computer screen.

"What happens now?"

"Well, he can't go near the shop until the AVO has been lifted," the officer replied. "It is for one year. In the meantime the matter will go to the small claims court. They will then get in touch with David about his hearing dates. He would be informed of these hearings in mail. The court will then reach a decision afterwards."

She said it with unmistakable clarity! David was doomed! But he was free to go for now once he signed the papers to show that he received the AVO and understood its terms and conditions and she promised him that she would come to the house after work that evening. The police officer handed him a copy of the paper work as soon as he signed them. Both Rhonda and David came out of the police station. They didn't talk as they walked towards the bus stop; Rhonda realized that her bus was already there so they made a dash for it. David hopped on the same bus as well as Rhonda and she promised him that she would come to the house today after work. Shrewd as it may be but this would also give her an alibi for meeting Chris in case Sam enquired about her whereabouts for that evening.

It was a city bound bus so David stayed on as he planned to go into the city but she got off when they arrived to her stop. Rhonda gave him a peck on the cheek and said good bye to him. She looked at the patches of clouds in the eastern sky with the bitter winds blowing quite rapidly. It seemed cyclonic. Rhonda wondered how their meeting was to take place in that venue. She decided to give Chris a call. She dialed the number but the mobile was turned off. Once Chris got the missed call he'd certainly call her back.

It was hard to focus that afternoon as she sat at her desk answering calls. A couple of hours later Rhonda looked out of the office window. Almost airborne! The gusty winds swept the dry leaves through in magnificently discordant patterns. The blue sky of the summer morning turned suddenly ashen with the distant palm trees standing quite still as the branches enthused frantically about, stuck to the tree, going nowhere! The storm wasn't brewing anymore! Indeed, it had started!

The mobile on the table suddenly rang to Bruno Mars's tune *just the way you are.* Rhonda picked it up and yes, it was Chris … finally. She answered the phone nervously, her hands shaking uncontrollably so that she nearly dropped it. But she answered it with her usual calmness.

"Hello, Chris how're you?" she said.

"Not too bad, and you?" Chris answered just as calmly. "Look, about that meeting tonight, why don't you come around to my place?"

"Yours!" Rhonda said aghast.

"Yes."

"But your family? Are they not going to be there?" Rhonda could not believe that Chris would make such an outrageous proposition.

"Yeah! But they are having a night out with friends. So we'll have the house to ourselves at least till midnight," Chris said.

" Are you sure?"

"Hundred percent. I'll wait from six 'o' clock onwards and my address is

62, Crescent Avenue

Greenvale Golf Course.

Rhonda penned down the address.

"Okay! I'll see you there," she said.

"See ye, Bye."

Rhonda looked at the address that had playground of the rich writ all over. She mulled over it, slightly mesmerized but made up her mind. Yes, she would go, no matter what! She didn't believe in the pecking order!

The mobile rang again. This time it was Sam asking her about David and her plans tonight. She said, he was fine and that she was going to tell him all about it once she got home, but she needed to be with David at the moment. Sam was convinced and didn't push it. Rhonda then called the transinfo to find out the bus routes from here. `Bit of a journey,' she thought. 'Quite arduous.' But she was determined to go. The storm had eased off slightly by now as she left for the five-thirty bus.

The bus stopped one street away from Chris's place. Rhonda got off. She sat down under the shade of the bus stop and opened her black bag which suddenly looked quite ugly and utterly daggy! Her outfit was not in vogue. Suddenly! Against this backdrop she wished she had bought something new for the occasion. She took her compact and her lipstick out to touch up and then had a close look at her skin and hair. Not bad for a fifty-two year old, she told herself! Then she put her belongings into the bag, flung it over her shoulder and took one confident step forward.

The memories of the last few days with Chris became vivid. He had called her one day to tell her that his medical team was going on a long excursion and that he was going with them as a trainee. They would be back in about a year's time but he would write to her. One whole year without seeing Chris, the young, restless Rhonda was devastated. She realized that this was just the beginning. Chris would be away on and off for the rest of their lives and that would be it. She remembered daddy! How he never came back! What if Chris did the same? One day he would go off on an excursion and never really come back! What would happen then? Rhonda got carried away, frightened and anxious. She stopped replying to the many letters he had written to her and then Chris also stopped writing one day!

By now Rhonda was already on Chris's drive way. She took a deep breath at the entrance of the massive house. She thought of her dingy little apartment and her dilapidated family home that needed renovations so badly! She stepped forward and walked past Chris's cherry red Ferrari parked on the drive way on the door step of the house. She rang the bell and waited! Moments went by and the butterflies in her stomach kept getting worse. Finally! There was sound on the other side of the door. The huge wooden door opened.

And yes! There he was! Chris! Her Chris!

Rhonda looked at him. For one incredible moment it seemed surreal! She pinched herself for a reality check.

"Rhonda!" Chris was saying.

"Yes! Chris, how's it going?" Rhonda said.

They spaced out for awhile staring at each other until Chris blinked and ushered Rhonda inside and shut the door behind them.

Episode 6

Chris held Rhonda by the waist and led her into the formal living room. He was close! So very close that she felt his breath on her back when they took their steps together like fluttering butterflies dancing in unison. The spacious living-room was tastefully decorated with expensive Victorian style furniture of burgundy velvet fabric for the upholstery. The heavy floral curtains matched the color of the sofa. Antic decoration pieces were placed casually on the centre table and the broad side tables. 'What would David do if he were here?' Rhonda thought miserably. A piano stood on the landing of the huge wooden staircase. Few pictures of Chris with a handsome woman were showcased every where in the room. Rhonda sat down on a high backed large single chair away from Chris, who sat opposite to her on a settee after he poured Rhonda a glass of red wine from a crystal canister from the bar on the far end of that large room.

"I'm glad that you could come!" Chris spoke first once the

awkward moments of enthralled silence passed. "Looks quite nasty! That storm."

"Winds' pretty strong too! But it slowed down by the time I started thankfully! Rhonda cleared her throat. "It was one of those short summer storms."

"I didn't see your car? Where're you parked?"

"Oh! I took the bus!"

Rhonda took a sip from the vintage wine.

"I see!"

Chris said moving his wine glass around in circles.

Rhonda could see that his hairline had receded showing signs of age on his sideburns. But he didn't bother to hide them. That boyish, bygone pristine look has now been replaced with this middle-aged appearance of deep furrows and stress marks. He spoke effortlessly in his usual charming manner that Rhonda always found so attractive.

"Why did you not answer my letters?"

Chris finally asked looking at her from his wine glass.

"I didn't see the point," she answered blankly.

"How do you mean?"

"Well you were gone! And were going to stay away for a long time! What was I to do in the meantime?"

"You could have come with me!"

Rhonda was quiet. How was she to tell him that she was afraid to accompany him into the jungles of Congo, the rainforests of Amazon, and the wetlands of the tropics on his research missions? How was she to convince him that she loved him,! loved him so and still does, in spite of it all?

"How did you meet her?" Rhonda gesticulated with her eyes.

"Who? O, Raisa," he said.

That's her name then? Raisa. Nice name!

"I met her in South Africa. She's a writer, has written quite a few books?"

Of all the books she'd read, how strange that she hadn't come across a single one of hers! She was jealous! Jealous that she couldn't be a writer; jealous that she couldn't be Chris' wife! Fate had played a dirty trick on her!

"And your son? When was he born?"

"He's not mine. I adopted him. He's Raisa's … from her

first marriage," he said.

"Oh, I see."

"I'm afraid he's a bit reckless with driving! Not a bad boy?"

Chris said and looked at her.

"I'm sure he isn't!"

"By the way tell Clara not to worry about the quotes. She can send the car to my garage and I'll pay for the damages," he said.

"Thank you! That's very generous. I'll most certainly give her the message."

Rhonda suddenly felt she was in uncharted territory. She was certain that she didn't want to … no she didn't! Want to be here anymore! Chris obviously had great respect for his wife. She felt strangely funny in her lower abdomen as her body cringed suddenly making her feel awkward. This was most unnatural, why was she even here? She shouldn't be! Really she shouldn't! She would breakdown eventually! But then as she looked outside, another storm had started with gushing winds, lightening and thunder. It was dark and forbidding! And she felt vulnerable at this moment to go anywhere by her self! But she tried anyway.

"I need to go home Chris. Do you think you could call me cab please?"

"I could but I don't think they'll come out in this weather! Look, I'll take you home shortly once the storm has passed," Chris paused. "Let's get dinner started, shall we? You must be starving by now, cause' I am!"

He stood up and gestured Rhonda with his hand to come with him into his very modern kitchen. Rhonda was going to cook dinner in Chris's kitchen with him! What were the odds of that happening? Seize the moment, Rhonda Smith, while you still can she told herself, for this was a one off.

Chris got Lettuce, Tomatoes, Cucumber, Mushrooms and Onions out of the fridge and gave them to Rhonda asking her to make a Salad. Rhonda stood quietly at the countertop while Chris brushed up and down her back as he went past grabbing the knife, the cutting board and the salad bowl over her shoulders. Rhonda smelt his strong odor from his after shave and felt his torso against her back as he did so. She had the salad underway, slicing the fresh vegetables while Chris got busy baking a large chicken roast.

"Have you any dressing?"

Rhonda asked feeling natural again once that confounded moment had passed.

"Yes! What dressing did you want?" Chris enquired. "I developed a taste for honey and mustard dressing while I was in South Africa, like to try some?"

Honey and mustard dressing? That didn't seem too appealing at all!

"How about the less exotic ones, the one's that we get here?"

"Sure! I don't see why not."

Chris accommodated straightaway handing her the continental dressing over his shoulder.

"Perfect! Thanks."

She poured some lavishly into the crystal bowl and whisked it about through the salad; it was ready when she put it on the table that Chris had just set with two red ribbed mats, white fine bone china dinner plates and salad bowls on top, cutlery on each side and two wine glasses. The cooking alarm went off for the chicken roast and Chris took it out of the European oven in one confident stride and carried it to the table.

"Walla! Let's eat," he said.

Rhonda could almost see the charming old Chris in him!

"Let's!"

"You know, you haven't really changed that much," he said.

"How do you mean?"

Rhonda asked cutting a drumstick from the roast.

"Well, you're still quite slim. Your large brown eyes look just the same under that burning brown hair! Exquisite!"

"Yes! I wish my life was just as enchanting as well!"

Chris looked straight at her across the table while Rhonda lowered her head towards the food. A lightening flashed outside causing power outage. Chris got up and grabbed the match box off the mantle piece and lighted the candles in the chandelier straight above them. Then he nodded slowly to what Rhonda said not moving his gaze from her face at all! He touched her face with his eyes, caressed it tenderly in the candle light as it bestowed softness to her already soft face.

Her large brown eyes sparkled today when she looked up to find him gazing down at her which finally fixed on her painted thin lips. He wooed her with his eyes and she smiled a sweet young smile to which he responded.

"Middle Eastern people are quite promiscuous, did you know that!" Chris said placing the napkin on his lap as he sat back on his chair cutting through the chicken breast with his knife.

"Really? Why?"

"Womanizing!" he said.

"But don't they marry them?"

"Yes! It still is womanizing! They just do so legally!"

"What about us? We are promiscuous too, aren't we?"

"Of course, but we render ourselves vulnerable to the world criticism more because we accept no legal responsibility! No strings attached."

"But wouldn't you say we've evolved as a liberal society rather than decadent or promiscuous, if you like?" Rhonda asked.

Chris pondered before he answered that and then finally said.

"Good question! The promiscuity in the Arab world, especially among men is incorporated into the culture and that somehow makes it moral! They will marry as many as four times once their wives have hit menopause, going for younger women and the society would condone it as long as they marry them," he said plainly. Again among the primitive tribes there is promiscuity as well but is not a moral issue for them because it is an instinctive choice as they don't know right from wrong!"

"Then why is it an issue for us?" Rhonda asked and then paused. "Are we morally bankrupt in the eyes of the world?"

"I'd say, since civilization has awakened us to morality, it is perhaps our obligation to exercise it more rigorously. Having multiple partners out of wedlock can be perceived as being decadent. We clothe ourselves knowing fully well exactly how much to reveal to make us sexually appealing which makes modesty a thing of the past. We might not quite see it that way, but we are still responsible for our moral conduct at end of the day!"

"To come back to your point then, it is okay for the primitive people because they remain untrained in these notions of bad or good while it's just the contrary for us!"

"Exactly right! What sets us apart from them is this awareness. It wouldn't be right for you to go out in the street without clothes because you have been tutored
over many generations that this is not appropriate, but for a primeval woman it would be perfectly fine simply because she wouldn't know better!"

"But what about the Arab men then? They too have moral obligation, don't they?"

"They do! That's why the marriages! Multiple may be! But they still take responsibility! For all the wives and that makes it okay," Chris paused thoughtfully. "Although, the world does acknowledge their roguishness just as well!"

The storm had passed by now and dinner was finished too. Electricity was back to normal. The antic clock said it was 10 'o' clock. Rhonda's mobile suddenly rang breaking the sanctity of their conversation; it was Sam.

"Where the heck are you? You are not with David, are you?" he snarled.

"How did you find out?"

"I didn't! I only asked and you answered me!"

"I'll be home soon," Rhonda said haltingly.

"I'll take you home now." Chris said somewhat gravely picking up the car keys from the side table.

"Yeah! That'd be nice!"

She looked at her mobile phone and called David. His phone was turned off. Rhonda frowned at that.

"Everything okay?" he asked.

"Yes, thanks everything's fine."

Rhonda answered swinging her bag over her shoulder.

The table was messy when Chris and Rhonda stepped outside. He turned the lights off and opened the door and closed it behind her. He then led her into the Ferrari and Rhonda sank comfortably into the leather passenger seat once he opened the front door for her. By now most of the clouds had dissipated and a hand full of stars was out in the calm sky of the dark breezy night. Rhonda looked at a CD cover lying on the dash board. It said, "The Jacaranda Blues" on the cover.

"Do you fancy Jazz?" Chris said getting in front of the wheels beside Rhonda. She nodded with a smile; Chris took the CD out of the cover and pushed it into the CD cavity. "It is a new South African Band."

"That's an unusual name for a band?" Rhonda said

"It is, isn't it?" Chris said, but there's a reason for it. The band master had said that he was downtrodden at one time and couldn't see the bright colors of life. Every thing looked dull, grey and dreary. That is why he calls it, "Jacaranda blues" in his misery he couldn't see the beauty of the lavender, all he saw was grey. He reversed the car as he spoke while Rhonda listened to the music in silence.

"Where do you live?" Chris suddenly asked.

"O, look just drop me off at the nearest train station please. I'll catch a train home."

"Are you sure?"

"Yes, quite sure," Rhonda said emphatically. "Besides, you need to clear the table; your wife would be home soon."

"I told her that I was having dinner with an old friend."

"You mean, she knows about us?"

'Not in so many words, but I think she can figure it out. She's smart."

He said looking at her from time to time.

"She doesn't mind?"

"Why should she?" Chris replied. "We're old friends! Aren't we not? The train's not safe this time of the night."

"Okay then, take me to 56, Bangalla street, Boondall," Rhonda gave up.

"No worries."

Chris said casually feeding it into the GPS. Rhonda suddenly felt dizzy! "Old friend!" 'Isn't that what he said?' "An old friend!" 'Oh! How could he!' She asked Chris to drive her to the bus stop at the Jacaranda tree. Chris didn't push it. They said good bye promising to meet again and kissed each other on the cheeks. Rhonda got out of the car, waited for him as he drove past her. She looked up at the Jacaranda tree and thought that the color of the flowers seemed pretty dull and ashen somewhat! Anyway, it was late so she hurried home as fast as she could. She went up the stairs and as she walked along the corridor, she had the oddest feeling. It felt ghastly! The dim lights illuminating in the stillness of the night! She could almost hear the music in the silent breathing of the people.

Chris hadn't touched her, not even once and he justified it but her chest was heaving…a pain most unforgettable! A memory that left her haunted, lonely!

She opened the door and crept inside as quietly as a church mouse. Sam's snoring was audible from here. The sound came and went in waves. She went into the study and found the pictures still lying on the floor from last night. They reminded her again of her predicament. Chris's reluctance wasn't from any moral raison d'être she knew, but age itself; Raisa was so much younger. Rhonda still had a pretty young smile because no matter what smiles never age! But it would have to be a platonic relationship, soul mates and that was certain from his behavior tonight. She turned off the lights and lay flat on her back on the carpet in the very clothes she had chosen with so much care that morning. It didn't matter anymore whether or not they got crumpled. She tossed and turned restlessly trying to sleep. Finally she dozed off with a heavy lump in her throat.

"David! David needs help! Rhonda cried as she talked in her sleep, "Mama! Don' cry. Don' cry Mama! Dad will be back. "Yes dad will be back sweetie! Everything will be okay! Everything!" Suddenly, two strong arms were around Rhonda picking her up like feather carrying her off and then gently putting her down in a soft bed. "Let me go! O! Let go of me! I don'need you, I don'need anyone. Chris! Sam, Sam …!"

Episode 7

David woke up early. He didn't mind that the AVO stopped him from going to work. But the thought of stealing money and subsequently squandering it didn't make him proud. He lit a cheap cigarette as he stood in the patio before sitting down in the old faded Ottoman with his flabby legs up on the chair. He didn't see Clara walking into the patio as he scratched his bristly beard on his round moon like face. His beefy forearms rested on the arms of the chair while his portly belly stuck out. He looked at Clara with his beady eyes and had a thin smile on his non-descript thick-lipped mouth under the chubby cheeks.

"What are you doing today?" she asked.

"Dunno, just bum'in around and wait'in for that court order," he said twisting the corner of his mouth.

"Can you do me a favor then?" she asked.

"Sure, sis, what do'ya want me t' do?"

"You'd got to take my car to Motorama at Indroo,"

"Why?" he asked curiously.

“Well apparently the boy’s dad is a big shot, a friend of Rhonda’s. He asked for it to be sent to his garage; they’ll take care of it,” she said.

“Great! No worries!”

“Tha.”

Clara turned around on her heels and left.

“When do’ye get off work today?” David asked suddenly.

“Same time,” Clara answered looking at him over her shoulder.

David turned his face and looked up at the sky. It was a bright sunny day. No work! That’s heavenly. He thought and smiled in a lazy sheepish way. He got to have some breakfast. There was milk in the fridge and cereal in the larder. He poured the milk out in a bowl from the dish rack that Clara had just washed before leaving. He found a spoon in the drawer and sat down at the kitchen counter. He turned on the TV before he began to eat. Flicking through the channels one after another, he found nothing interesting so he switched it off and picked up the spoon. The phone rang. It was Mike.

“Hey Mike! What’s up?” David asked

"I need money, man," he said.

"I can't give you any? I am grounded! Big time man! Big time!"

"You got to get us the blomin' money. We got to get us stoned!" Mike cried.

"I got to get my weed too! But I am busted! I told ye!" David said.

"Someone's at the door. I got to go."

David hung up and rushed to open the front door.

"Rhonda! Aren't you at work?" David said.

"I took the day off to be with you."

"That's awfully nice!"

"Can I come in?"

"Sure thing! But I got go out in a while."

"Where?"

"Got to take Clara's's car to her garage."

"O Yeah? I'll come with you."

"Why? Don't you trust me?"

David asked looking at Rhonda with his lips turned up and a deep frown between his brows.

“It’s not about trust David!” Rhonda said pushing her way inside the house, her mother’s house, their family home. “You need help darl! I want you to see a counselor!”

“A counselor? What’s a bloody counselor going to do for me? I need money! That’s what I need!”

“That’ll come too,” Rhonda said. “Later.”

“I need it now!”

“Why now? Don’t you have enough to eat at home?”

Rhonda asked raising her voice in apprehension.

“It’s got nothin’ to do with food.”

David said in a low voice.

“What has it got to do with then? I hope you are not turning into a mad punter just like daddy?”

“No! You will not understand! But I’m not going to a bloomin’ shrink?”

Try me! Rhonda said inwardly taking a deep breath but didn’t push it. What ever was going on, she was concerned for David. He definitely needed help. She might be better off talking to Chris about it. He was a psychiatrist, wasn’t he? Surely, he’d find a way to help David!

"Let's go to Indroo then? We'll go to Maccas from there."

David snickered at that but Rhonda pretended not to see. He had been neglected, misguided; he needed to see a proper psychiatrist! Rhonda would make sure this time that he didn't re-offend.

Sam waited for Rhonda when she came back in the evening. He had many questions but didn't get around talking to her yet. She went to bed early and had left early in a hurry. He had dismal thoughts about Rhonda keeping him in the dark about David's police case and who was Chris? Where was she last night when the storm broke out? The phone rang and Sam picked it up. It was Rhonda.

"I won't be coming home tonight."

"Where will you be?"

"I need to stay home with Clara, Emily and David."

"Why? What's wrong?" Sam asked.

"I can't tell you now."

This will have repercussions she knew. But she soldiered on. She simply didn't have the time or the tolerance for Sam's lectures now. David was her priority and it was him who needed to be sorted out first.

"Well! O'right then! But you owe me an explanation! Don't you think?" Sam said grudgingly.

"You got to trust me on this one Sam," Rhonda hung up.

Sam looked at the receiver in his fist for a dumbfounded moment and then hung up with a bang.

"Damn it!"

Soon after she hung up, Rhonda thought she would get dinner started. There was some flour in the larder and potatoes. She thought she would make a shepherds pie. As soon as she started the sisters came home one after another, first Clara then Emily. They were overjoyed that Rhonda was sleeping over tonight. David stayed in his room, moping and had not come out for the rest of the evening. At dinner time it was just Clara, Emily and Rhonda at the table. Clara adjusted her spectacles on her sharp nose looking at Rhonda with her clear blue eyes. Her cropped black hair was brushed backwards showing a broad forehead. Her thin determined red lips set above the square chin, moved slightly together as she ate.

"I am taking David to see a psychiatrist soon," Rhonda said.

"Who are you taking him to?" Emily asked.

"Dr. Chris Saunders."

"What makes you think he can help him? They couldn't help me!" Emily said.

"Your case is too hard to treat, Emily," Clara said.

"Why?"

"Because you think you are fat when you are not. Those anti-depressants and counseling sessions won't treat Bulimia!" Clara said.

"Physicians can't help you Emily! But I believe we can?" Rhonda said.

"How?"

"By being supportive?"

"But I'm not getting any better! I have more hair in my body than ever before! Look at my scalp! I'm bolding!" she cried.

Emily got up from her chair not touching much food at all. She ran to her room on her rickety legs under that curved bony body and banged the door as she shut it. The Shepherd pie wasn't distasteful but it failed to interest Emily. Apart from the noise of the cutlery on the plate there was silence otherwise as Rhonda and Clara quietly ate away.

"Who's going to bear David's expenses?" Clara asked.

"I still need to sort that out."

Rhonda contemplated as Clara chatted away. The doctors and the psychiatrists couldn't cure Emily! David was going to seek help privately which Emily didn't but would even they be able to help him? She finished dinner and went to the living room to call Chris while Clara cleared the table. She went straight for Chris's number on the mobile as she sat comfortably in the grey, old sofa in the living room. His phone rang out. Hopefully he would call back soon, Rhonda thought.

As soon as she hung up, she heard the front door open and close. She found her bag in the kitchen countertop to put the mobile back in there. Suddenly, she realized that her purse inside her bag was open. She looked into it to check if anything was missing and yes! Her fifty dollar note was gone! She ran to David's room and knocked on the door but no! There was no sound! She quietly turned the knob to open the door. With the door ajar she looked at the messy bed, but David was nowhere! She crept inside slowly into the empty room and wrinkled her nose. There was an odor; a pungent smell! The room was smelly! Oh! The horrible smell of pot! And cigarette! Has he been smoking weed? Rhonda felt disgusted. She ran out of the room and went to Clara's.

"Nothin'ever changes in this miserable, sloppy, dump of a house!" Rhonda cried.

"What do you mean?"

"What da' I mean? I mean David."

"What's wrong?"

"Did you or you or anyone in this stupid! Stupid house know that our brother …David is hooked?"

"What!"

Emily screamed from the threshold of her bedroom door.

Rhonda sat down on the kitchen stool and started to cry. Emily and Clara stood in the middle of the kitchen astounded. They were thinking Hashish, Cocaine, Marijuana and so on …

"How did you find out?" Clara said.

"Do you even bother to go to his room?" Ever? When did you last do that? I bet never in the last five years," Rhonda lamented. “And now we have lost him! Lost him forever ...”

Moments passed and not one person in the room spoke. Emily started to sob suddenly. She sat down on the floor in her baggy clothes and wailed. Her hiccups became frightening as she choked close to having fits.

“When mum was alive, I warned him not to steal food from the larder. But David, a growing boy couldn’t help it! He grumbled and said, ‘But I’m always hungry, dinner doesn’t fill me up, no more!’ You do remember! Rhonda, don’t you? How we went to bed hungry! Every single night? There was never enough to eat, was there?”

So true! Rhonda nodded.

“And when David stole milk money to buy food and games, I warned him again and again … and stood up for him every time mum caught him,” Emily said relatively composed.“But David never changed.”

Suddenly the mobile rang. Rhonda made a dash for her bag and fumbled around for the phone. It was Chris.

“Hello Chris, how are you?”

Rhonda answered bleakly.

"Good! And you?"

"Not too bad."

"What's happened?"

"I needed to speak to you about a problem!"

"Sure! Why not come by to my clinic after five one day? And we'll talk."

"How about tomorrow?"

"Tomorrow's fine," Chris said and hung up.

"We need to have Chris over for dinner one day," Clara said to Rhonda biting her nail nervously, "he has been awfully nice, hasn't he?"

"And what's the likelihood of that happening? You are eternally optimistic aren't you?"

That night David didn't return. Nobody knew where he was. His mobile was left in the house and there was no way to find him!

Episode 8

Next morning when Sam was getting ready for his jog, he heard a sound of the key turning into the key hole in the front door. He stood in the middle of the room as the door slowly opened. Sam stared at the door bewildered; he still couldn't see the intruder. When the door opened a bit, he walked a few steps towards it. It was David! He strolled into the room in disheveled clothes, untidy hair and looked at Sam like a mouse lured into a trap for cheese.

"Hey! What are you up to? Sam said. You gave me such a shock!"

"I am messed up man, really screwed!"

"How so?"

"May I sit down?"

"Of course!"

Sam thought he was going to miss his jog anyway so might as well have breakfast with David at the kitchen counter. He got two earthenware bowls out of the cupboard and poured some cornflakes into David's bowl with milk and took another for himself. They sat next to each other as David gulped huge spoonfuls of it in silence with Sam looking on from the corner of his eyes.

After they finished Sam asked.

"You wanted to say something?"

Sam had been in the dark all this time and he couldn't hold his curiosity any more. And David thought Sam could help him if he would be patient enough to hear him out! He trusted him because he was family! He trusted him because he wasn't judgmental!

Sam listened patiently as David took him aboard on the rollercoaster trip of his life. And now that the beans were spilled and David was purged at last, Sam sat on the stool, somber; enraged! Not sure of his verdict yet!

"*I* want the kind of help that *I* need! Not the kind that *they* think *I* need!"

David said as the cathartic moment ended.

"What do you mean?"

"Rhonda wants me to go to this rich friend of hers. I believe he is a psychiatrist?"

"Really!"

"Why, didn't you know?"

"No!"

"Well tell her that I don't want to!"

"And why not?"

"Because, my friend, Mike tried it all … counselling, rehab, the works man! The works! But he is back in the dungeon," David said as he pursed his mouth. "With me!"

David and his cohort moved in together obviously and they do not want to be found. All the help that David wanted was money and the only person in the world he trusted was Sam. The addicts had arrived to a stage where their own parents were buying them drugs or else they would perish. That was what Mike's mum did sometimes! She went to the dealers herself to buy drugs for Mike, just to see him alive! Not well, but alive! The police didn't know about it! They didn't have to! They might know the underworld but could they cure addiction?

David dropped the key on the sofa.

“These are Rhonda’s,” he said in a low subdued voice and then continued. “I took them when I stole her money … the fifty dollars. I’ll pay her back some day.”

“Pay her back! Do you even realize what you’ve got yourself into?” Sam said looking furiously at David and holding him by the shoulder in an iron grip and shaking him violently.

“I’d, I really would … wa …one day,” David stammered. “You are hurting me Sam! Get your hands off me! Or else…”

“Yeah? Or else what! Call the coppa!”

But Sam’s grasp tightened as David cowed in weakness. All his struggles came to naught and then suddenly with one cowardly rage he dug his teeth deep into his hands and Sam, instead of releasing him took the knife impulsively from the sink and lounged it at him jabbing it through his shoulder.

“What the! David screamed. “Sam … oh, no! Please Sam! It hurts aauoch …” But his feeble muscles slowly relaxed, his jaw fell apart and he fell, unconscious on the floor in a pool of his own blood! Awful, Oh! How awful it was!

‘O my goodness! What have I done? Where do I hide? What do I do?’ Sam panicked and stumbled over David’s comatose body as he ran! He leapt over the flights of stairs until he reached the road in front of the apartment block. He kept running and running and never looking back, not even once until he deClarad himself a fugitive as he disappeared over the horizon.

In the meantime a neighbor called an ambulance and Rhonda was asked to come home from work, Emily came sobbing and so did Clara. David's body was taken to the morgue and that was that! David's life had been a waste but Rhonda's only comfort was that one day he would have overdosed himself to death anyway. Poor David! He never really got a chance! Did he? And Sam? Did he get a chance? Does he deserve society's sympathy? Or its condemnation? Rhonda cried, Emily cried, and Clara tuned into ABC for news update.

Her phone rang soon after and it was Chris. He witnessed the great tragedy, as it were, on TV and as Shakespearean audience saw how this actor had his exit from the world's theatre! His condolences to the grieving family fell on deaf ears as the lamenting Rhonda broke down into uncontrollable tears! These were tears of sorrow, of joy, of empathy and of self pity entwined into one flowing rivulet of boundless outburst. Chris gave Rhonda a few minutes, mumbled a goodbye, and then hung up.

Episode 9

Autumn followed in as summer passed and the landscape slowly changed. Their moods also changed with the passing season, although Sam was never found. The new season brought pestilence of multi-colored dry leaves on the walkway which Rhonda crunched up one morning while she sauntered into an orphanage.

The sale sign was finally put up on their family home and the remaining siblings moved in with her. But as time went by, they realized that the place felt empty and that they ought to do something about it. So they decided to adopt a child from the orphanage to raise it as their own with Rhonda being the applicant.

The children lined up for her that morning on the command of their supervisor, Mrs Jenings. She took Rhonda's application and should it be approved then she could select any child. The selection could start right now. This was awful! Rhonda thought as she looked at them standing next to one another in a row of human cargo ready for a transaction; children in tattered clothes, innocent, wide eyed, melancholy and afraid! Rhonda's pick, however, wasn't among them … the one that she had singled out on the bus one midsummer afternoon! She described the child to Mrs Jenings and after much hesitation she said there was a problem.

"What was the problem?" Rhonda asked.

"Well! The child has a disability," she said to Rhonda. "She has Autism."

"What of that?"

"That's why she was returned!"

"What happens when nobody wants them?"

'They remain in the custody of the state," she grimaced.

Unloved, and in neglect, their life perishes without much hope of happiness.

"No!" Rhonda decided. "That's the child I want! That's whom I'll adopt!"

"Okay! Perhaps, your application will then be approved sooner?" Mrs Jenings replied.

The application was approved and Rhonda went to the

orphanage on time to collect the child. She even had a name for her – Cherubs! And Cherubs steadily became a member of the family. It was quite dramatic how she altered Rhonda's life with her ubiquitous presence! Rhonda went shopping with her. She went to the bookstores with her as she looked for books, to read to her, to share with her! And the Jacarandas? Next summer, they blossomed in infinite profusion with the petals skewing down the westerly winds in lilting lovely lavender! The blues were suddenly gone!

CPSIA information can be obtained at www.ICGtesting.com
Printed in the USA
BVOW08s1016301115

428866BV00001B/85/P

9 781462 640904